I0571153

Wife for the Crowd

OTHER BOOKS IN THE WIFE-TO-BE SERIES

Wife without a Ring
Wife Insurance
Wife Next Door
Wife with a Plan
Wife for a Day
Wife Envy
Wife Again
Wife.Edu

Wife for the Crowd

A WIFE-TO-BE NOVELLA

A'NDREA J. WILSON

Divine Garden Press

Wife for the Crowd is a work of fiction. All incidents and dialogue, and all characters with the exception of some well-known historical figures and public figures are products of the author's imagination and are not to be construed as real. Where real life historical or public figures appear, the situations, incidents, and dialogues concerning those persons are entirely fictional and are not intended to depict actual events or to change the entirely fictional nature of the work. In all other retrospects, any resemblance to persons living or dead is entirely coincidental.

Wife for the Crowd. Copyright ©2015 by A'ndrea J. Wilson. All Rights Reserved. No part of this book may be used or reproduced by any means without written permission from the author with the exception of brief quotations in printed reviews.

Published by Divine Garden Press, LLC
P.O. Box 371
Soperton, GA 30457
www.divinegardenpress.com

ISBN-13: 978-0692455081
ISBN-10: 0692455086

Cover Design & Interior Layout by Divine Lit Services
www.divinelit.com

Above all, love each other deeply, because love covers over a multitude of sins.

(1 Peter 4:8, NIV)

Look at All These Rumors

Davina

"We have a problem."

The silky, deep, masculine voice of my manager causes my eyes to flutter open. Rick isn't a morning person, so if he's calling me at—I roll over in my bed and peer at my alarm clock—8:49 a.m., there is definitely epic news. The word PROBLEM gets stuck in my head and makes me feel weak. I am scared to open my mouth and ask, "How bad is it?" I get a visual of my record label pulling my upcoming album and shredding my recording deal. They wouldn't do that six weeks before the release date . . . would they?

"Davina," Rick calls to me. "Davina, are you still there? Davina, wake up!"

"I'm up. I'm up." I moan and pull my lavender comforter over my head. "I just don't want to know what the problem is. Let me sleep for two, no three more hours. Then let me wake up on my own, take a shower, get dressed, have a cup of green tea, and read the paper before you ruin my day with whatever this problem is all about. Let me enjoy a few more hours of stardom before you take it all away."

I hear him chuckle. "Davina Lacey, stop being such a diva. You're so dramatic. Sometimes, I think you should have gone into acting rather than singing."

I look up at my comforter from underneath it. Natural light floods into my bedroom from the large bay window and seeps through the cotton fabric, illuminating the comforter. Even hiding under the covers doesn't give me the dark retreat that I crave. I push aside the comforter and sit up in my bed, considering new career options. Rick could be onto something. Acting might not be so bad. "After you tell me the problem, I'll probably have ample time to pursue another career. I guess becoming an actress wouldn't be the end of the world. Maybe I could do a few musicals. I mean, I'd still get a chance to sing. Plenty of gospel artists have done musicals . . . after their careers start to die."

He lets out a frustrated groan. "Would you be quiet and let me tell you the problem? It's pretty bad, but it's not what you think."

I sigh. There's no way of running from this news, and Rick is not going to prolong the announcement as I've requested. I have no choice but to brace myself for the worst. "Alright. Go on and break my heart." I imagine that I'm Toni Braxton in the "Unbreak My Heart" video, sobbing uncontrollably over my dead boyfriend who has just been in a motorcycle accident—except in my daydream, my unreleased CD and a Grammy award are smashed into pieces on the tar pavement instead of a wounded man. Plus, I don't have a boyfriend in real life anyway.

Rick is silent for a few seconds, allowing my imagination to run wild for too long, then he says, "They think you're gay."

It's early in the morning—at least according to my typical schedule it is—so my mental processing of his words feels slow and delayed. "What? You mean gay as in happy?"

He snickers. "No, gay as in homosexual. They think you're a lesbian."

My right hand shoots up to my neck as if I am wearing pearls—which I am not—and now clutching them. "Who thinks I'm a lesbian? The record label?"

"No, the public."

"Rick," I whine. "Why would they think that?"

He lets out another laugh. I can't believe he finds any of this the least bit amusing. He then clears his throat and says, "Sorry. There's a rumor floating around. Someone who claims to know you is saying that the reason you aren't in a relationship and have never been seen with a date at events is because you're not into men."

I gasp. *Why are people telling lies about me? Who is this so-called informant who's slandering my name?* "A rumor? Who's behind this rumor? And how did you hear about it?"

"I don't know who started it, but it's gone viral. It's all over social media—Facebook, Twitter, GooglePlus. There are huge debates happening about it. Some people are showing support while others feel it's an abomination. Several articles from websites with absolutely no credibility are floating around. But you know, people don't care about validity anymore. They hear some gossip and just spread it without checking the facts. I even heard one of the Christian radio stations were discussing it during their morning show today."

I feel like crying. I never want to leave my apartment again—like Rick would ever let that happen. How did I go from rising star to rumor mill? "I just don't understand, Rick. When did all of this happen?"

"I guess the first article came out sometime yesterday and then it began circulating. Spread like fire. We have to move quickly on this thing and do some serious damage control. I know you're used to staying up late and sleeping in, but this morning, I need you to get up and meet me at LifeStory Records. There's a meeting at 11 o'clock and you're required to be there."

I groan. "Do I have to?"

"Yes, you have to. Stop sulking and get going. If you care anything about your career as a Gospel artist, you'll be there on time and willing to do whatever it takes to clear up this matter."

Despite my complaints and overall lethargic mood, I make it to LifeStory Records on-time, with five minutes to spare. A receptionist greets me and I am led down the hallway and into a small conference room. When I enter the room, I am surprised to see that I am the last one to arrive. A few of the label's executives are present, along with my manager, Rick Williams, some woman I've never seen before, and . . . is that Kenny Kauffman?

Rick stands and welcomes me with a hug. He's more than a manager to me—he's my cousin, and he always shows me love. "Good girl," he whispers in my ear and pats me on top of my head as if I'm a puppy. I pull back to shoot him an evil glare, but he halts my response by saying, "Davina, you already know Mr. Bradley, Mr. Short, and Ms. Thompson."

He's referring to the label execs. I give them a courteous nod of acknowledgement.

Rick moves his eyes to the woman I don't know. "And this is Nora Locke. She'll be assisting us with your . . . situation."

Situation? It's obvious that the powers that be have already decided how they're going to handle my *situation.* Forget about any ideas I have—I don't have any ideas but that's not the point. The point is that these people always think they know what's best for me before I have a chance to think about what's best for me. If I hadn't worked so hard to get to where I'm at, I would tell them all to kick rocks and storm out of the place. Instead, I offer Nora a faux smile.

"And, you probably recognize Grammy-winning recording artist, Kenny Kauffman. He's the one who sings—"

"I know what he sings," I says tersely to Rick. "Nice to meet you, Kenny. Are we supposed to do a duet or something?"

"A duet. That's a good idea," Mr. Short says.

Oh Lord. If Kenny is at the meeting to save me from these homosexual rumors and it's not because they were planning for us to do a duet, I'm really nervous about what tricks the execs have up their sleeves. I take a seat in the chair that Rick ushers me to, the chair next to Kenny. I'm trying not to look as anxious as I feel. I tell myself over and over that I am a professional and that I can handle whatever is put before me. Bad press comes with the territory. I'm a celebrity with a platinum album and two Grammys. On the Gospel side of the music industry, that's huge. Most Gospel/Contemporary Christian albums don't even reach gold status. My first album went platinum, selling over a million copies, and they're expecting my second album to do even better—if this crazy rumor doesn't kill my career first.

"I'm sure Rick has filled you in on the nasty gossip that is spreading about your sexual orientation," Ms. Thompson says.

I frown. "Unfortunately, he has."

"Is there any truth to it?" she probes.

I can't help but feel offended. "Excuse me?"

She smiles politely. "We have to ask before we take action."

I roll my eyes. "No. It's not true."

Mr. Bradley interjects, "The reason people believe that you could be homosexual is because you've never been seen out with a man who wasn't related to you or working with you."

"I'm focused on my career. I don't have time for a boyfriend. When did it become a sin to be single?" I hate that I have to explain my lack of a man.

"It's not a sin to be single, but the Christian community can be very . . . particular," Mr. Bradley says. "As a celebrity, people want to make sure you're the real deal—that you're practicing what you preach. You saw how the Christian community went wild when Erica from Mary Mary wore that tight, white dress on her album cover. Christian celebs are held to a higher standard. They want to see you married with children, sort of like a politician or a pastor. You have to appear to be the role."

He was right. The media and church folks were in a frenzy over Erica Campbell. Who knew a turtleneck dress could cause such disruption? But I'm not Erica and I don't have a white, spandex dress in my closet. Moreover, nothing scandalous is in my closet, and I am sure not coming out of it. "There are plenty of Christian celebrities that aren't married," I say, confidently.

"But their success is limited. Name one extremely successful, single Christian artist who is not or was not part of a group," he challenges.

My mind goes blank. I am sure that there is somebody who meets this description, but as I scroll through my mental rolodex of crossover artists I love, all of them are indeed married—and to someone of the opposite sex.

Mr. Bradley grins when I don't immediately offer a response.

"Kierra Sheard," I desperately say, knowing that I won't get very much support for this argument.

Mr. Bradley offers me an unimpressed glance. "Yes, Kierra has done well, but she also comes from a famous gospel family—you don't."

I shrink in my seat.

Mr. Bradley obviously takes my reaction as defeat and continues to lay out the master plan. "Despite changes in our society related to same sex marriages, certain groups continue to uphold male-female relationships as sacred. Christians, for the most part, are one of these groups. Being a non-religious record label, we couldn't care less about your personal preferences, but because you are a religious artist and we have a lot of money invested into you, we need for you to make your sexual orientation crystal clear to world."

I'm really not interested in hashing out the details of my personal life and decision to remain single to the public, but if it will save my music career, I'll say what needs to be said. "So you want me to do a press conference or something like that, right?" I look around at everyone at the table, waiting—no hoping—for some level of comradery.

They are all on the same team all right . . . just not my team.

"Not exactly. We want you to get engaged," Ms. Thompson says, folding her hands in front of her as if it's a done deal.

Are these people insane? I look over at Rick, my manager, my *cuzzo*, the person who so-called has my back, and his eyes tell me that he agrees with them. *And you think you know someone. I'll fix him. I'm going to tell my Aunt Christie on him.*

I shake my head defiantly. "That's not going to happen. I just told you that I don't have time for a relationship. And even if I started dating soon, I wouldn't be engaged for a while. It would take time to meet the right person and get to know him."

Ms. Thompson smiles brightly like she's about to tell me I just won a new car. "Precisely! That's why we've taken all of the guesswork out of it. Meet your new fiancé, Kenny Kauffman."

I gasp. I must be in *The Twilight Zone* or on *Candid Camera*. I look around suspiciously, and when I don't see anything out of place, I say, "Fiancé? No way! Kenny? No disrespect, Kenny, but I don't even know you. Why would I marry him?"

Mr. Short speaks up. "We didn't say you had to marry him, at least not now. You two just need to be engaged for the sake of publicity. It'll instantly clear up the gay rumors and it will increase record sales for the both of you."

A minute ago, full disclosure to the world seemed frightening, but now, I wish the plan was as simple as that. "Why can't I just make an announcement? Why can't I just say it's all a big misunderstanding?"

"People won't believe you," Mr. Bradley says firmly. "Some might, but many will continue to question you. By the time this thing blows over, your record sales will be in the toilet. We don't have time to explain your ways to the public. We have to move quickly and we have to do something so big that it will destroy every single doubt lingering in your fans' minds."

I rub my temples. This entire situation is out-of-control. "I know this is bad, but I'm sure that this rumor cannot be so problematic that I have to fake an engagement just to sell records."

Mr. Bradley, seemingly tired of my opposition, says, "You wanna bet? Rick, please show her."

Rick, who is sitting on the other side of me, opens up a large laptop that rests on the table between us. After clicking a few tabs, he brings up several websites, all filled with discussions about me and my love life. One even has a picture of a random Latino woman who had taken a picture with me at an event and was now speculated to be my lover. *Really?*

The tweets are overwhelming. I actually have my own trending hashtag: #DavinaComesOut. *I can't believe this is happening to me.*

Rick then pulls up a chart of my album's presales which have dropped 50 percent in 24 hours. I don't want to accept it, but my problem is much worse than I imagined. Having my career taken away because people just don't receive my work is one thing, but having it taken away over a lie is completely different. I can't let some liar steal everything I've worked my rear end off to achieve.

I look at Rick with wild and frantic eyes. Telepathically, I want him to sense my desperation and tell me what to do. I guess we're on the same page because he nods at me, non-verbally encouraging me to go along with the label's plan. I look over at Kenny who seems calm, at little too calm if you ask me, considering the fact that he has just as much to lose as I do if this fake engagement is ever discovered.

"What are they offering you?" I ask him.

"Think of this as a favor from me to you," Kenny says coolly, but I know he's pretending. He doesn't know me to do me any favors. There's something that he wants, and going along with this plan is going to get it for him.

I laugh though nothing's remotely funny. "I'm not buying that. I need to know the truth before I agree to anything. What do you stand to gain?"

He shrugs. "I get good publicity, increased record sales, another album—pretty much everything you're getting. I'm doing it because it's good for my career. It's good for yours, too."

The execs are watching me. They know I'm going to give in, yet I have a moral dilemma. I'm a Christian and I hate to lie. Lying is a sin and every sin is the same—it's all sin. My lie is just as bad as the lies that have been told about me, and technically, my lie is just as bad as homosexuality. The Christian community might not want a gay gospel artist, but they don't want a liar either, so why am I really about to cave in to this mass deception of me marrying Kenny?

Because if you don't, you'll lose it all.

I offer them a weak nod. I can't say the words, but it's understood that I am agreeing to their plan. *Forgive me, Lord.*

"Perfect," Mr. Bradley says. "Nora is a media whiz and she will be attached to the both of you over the next several weeks to ensure that the news of your engagement reaches the far ends of the earth. Get used to seeing her around."

I sigh in submission and mumble, "So, what's next?"

Ms. Thompson lays the palms of her hands flat against the table. "Well, now that we have everyone on board, it's time for Kenny to propose."

He Proposed . . . Sort Of

Davina

Less than two hours after my meeting with the label execs, I am in a private studio and my proposal is being staged. I feel like I'm making a music video rather than getting engaged. Wardrobe has dressed me in a pair of cute designer jeans, red bottom heels, and an off the shoulder, white blouse with a red belt. My hair and makeup are flawless, and I look way too trendy to be supposedly hanging out in the studio, working on a new track. If this was for real, I'd be caught in a pair of comfy sweatpants and a cotton tee with my hair pulled back in my signature ponytail, but I guess that wouldn't make for good P.R.

Everything in place, Kenny goes along with the program, interrupting my studio time to ask me for my hand in marriage. Obediently, I blush, pretend to be shocked, and say yes like a woman truly in love. Nora is there filming the whole thing on her camera phone. We end our *occasion* by taking several *perfect-happy couple* photos with me showing off my new $250,000 ring. The ring is the only part of the deal that I actually enjoy. The label must really want our engagement to look authentic because they've forked over a pretty penny for my jewelry. Too bad I'll have to return it when the jig is up.

Since I'm not the kind of woman who is obsessed with getting married, I'm not bothered by the fact that none of this charade is true. The only thing that bothers me is the mountain of lies that I'll rack up as I participate in this scheme. I guess Kenny is completely unaffected because when Nora has all the proof she needs and dismisses us, Kenny gives me a nonchalant shrug and exits the room.

As I head home, I wonder if this act will work and if Nora's as good as the execs claim. By the time I wake up the next morning—closer to afternoon—my questions are answered. Social media is a frenzy over the proposal, my engagement ring, and our perfect-happy couple photos. The execs were right. Not only is Nora a beast at getting the word out, no one dares to question my sexuality—outside of the typical skeptics and conspiracy theory folks.

Speaking of Nora, I am just getting ready to take my usual afternoon nap when she calls me. I'm not sure how she got my cell phone number, considering I never gave it to the label, but a process of elimination points the finger of blame at Rick.

"What can I do for you?" I ask, trying to sound sweet and polite, but on the inside feeling annoyed that she's keeping me away from my beauty sleep. If you haven't already figured it out, I sleep a lot. I need a total of ten to twelve hours of sleep throughout the day to keep me going. I often stay up late—hey, that's the life of a musician—but I still make sure to get at least eight hours of shut eye at night, then catch a few hours of Z's during the day. I'm not lazy; I'm just a sleeper. Some people are eaters, some are TV watchers; I'm a sleeper. It's my favorite thing to do next to singing, and I'm really good at it.

"You can meet me at Kenny's condo in two hours. I'll text you the address," she says, then hangs up before I can refuse the invite.

I scream in frustration. If I ever get my hands on this so-called source that started this ugly rumor about me, I will strangle him or her—Christ-like or not.

I'm late. Nora said two hours. It's two hours and twenty minutes later when I pull my Jaguar into Kenny's condo entrance. As I step out of the car in front of the valet, I notice a few photographers attempting to snap pictures of me. I'm sure Nora is behind the tip that I'd be arriving at Kenny's at this hour. Gospel artist don't usually have loads of paparazzi following them unless there's an event or emerging story. I guess the rumors, mixed with the engagement to Kenny, make the latter true for me, pushing me into the media limelight for all of the wrong reasons.

I shield my face with my black leather purse and quickly make my way into the building, and then onto the elevator. I press the button for Kenny's floor—twelve—and smile to myself, impressed that he's on the top level. *A penthouse condo. Way to go, Kenny.* I just hope he doesn't have an over-the-top, Cribs style, interior designed, but nonfunctional living space. Just because celebs make a little money doesn't mean that we have to become so cliché. With the exception of a few designer labels added to my wardrobe, I'm still the same down-to-earth *sistah* that I was three years ago when I signed my record contract.

I ride the elevator for less than a minute and step out into the hallway on the twelfth floor. There are two residences on this level, one to the left and one to the right. Kenny's is to the right—1202—so I walk to his door and ring the bell. He answers within seconds, appearing unintentionally attractive. Kenny is a heartthrob. He's one of those people who wake up looking like a million bucks while the rest of us have to prep and primp for an hour to be sort of cute. I'll be the first to admit that I am a total knockout on my album cover and promotional material, but my fabulousness only occurs after a few professional hair, makeup, and fashion stylists take me into their cave and create an image that I'm even surprised to see when I look into the mirror. But Kenny is *au naturel.* No makeup, no stylists, no glitz or glam. Just a haircut once a week, a few pieces of expensive jewelry, and whatever clothing he decides to throw on. I swear, the man could put on a pair of high-water jeans and an ugly Christmas sweater and still look magazine cover ready.

"Kenny," I say in the best indifferent tone I can muster up.

"What's up?" he asks as he moves aside and invites me into his domain. Once again, I'm impressed. His condo is tastefully decorated, but still feels lived-in. There's an oversized sectional sofa in the middle of his living room, and I can't help but to stroll over to it and plop down as if I'm at home.

"Have a seat," he says with a grin.

"Very funny. Where's Nora?"

He shrugs. "Your guess is as good as mine."

I sigh. As handsome as Kenny is, I really don't have time to hang out at his place. There's so much that I need to do before my album drops. I have a bunch of tour dates coming up and I really need to rehearse with the background singers. I should be doing radio and TV interviews right now, not fooling around playing house with Kenny Kaufman. "Can you call her and find out what's the hold up?"

He takes a seat across from me, whips out his cell phone, and dials Nora, putting the phone on speaker mode so that I can hear the conversation. She answers on the third ring.

"Hey, Kenny. Did Davina make it yet?"

He smiles at me. *Lady killer.* "Yeah, she's here. We're just waiting on you."

"Good. I'm not coming."

I gasp and yell, "What do you mean you're not coming?"

I can hear her laughing on the other end of the line. "You two are supposed to be the happy couple. Why would I be going out on a date with you? I've made reservations in Kenny's name at Bleu. Just keep your receipt and the label will reimburse you for the meal."

"I doubt either of us is worried about paying for dinner," Kenny says.

I glare at him and say, "Speak for yourself." I hate when people try to count my money. I refuse to end up as a has-been, broke celebrity because I squandered my earnings on dinners at overpriced restaurants with fake fiancés. "Nora, what are we supposed to do without you?"

I hear her let out a deep sigh. How can she be flustered with me when I'm the one flustered with her? "Uh, how about eat? And oh yeah, have fun and let the paparazzi get a few good photos of you two together."

"But—"

"No buts," she says. "This is a simple dinner, so don't mess it up. Ciao!"

The line goes dead. I look up at Kenny who seems completely unfazed.

"So, what now?" I ask, feeling extremely vulnerable and uncomfortable.

He stands up. "I say we go eat. I'm hungry and I hear they have good steaks. I'll drive."

Guess Who's Coming to Dinner

Kenny

It's **refreshing to meet** a woman like Davina. A perk of being a successful, single, music artist is that I have a lot of available women—and unavailable women—throwing themselves at me. Getting a date or being seen with a beautiful female is as easy as breathing. I remember the days before the fame when I had to actually try to impress a woman. At the time, I thought it was a bit taxing to figure out the right thing to say or do, but now that it's so simple, I sort of miss the chase. Getting something without effort definitely changes its perceived value. I often find myself turned off by ladies who walk in desperation like shoes. It's a rare occurrence to meet a woman who either isn't interested or at least is good at playing the hard to get role. I realize this is the exact reason why I find Davina Lacey so appealing. Don't get me wrong, she's a very talented and beautiful person, but her singular focus on her career and not a man awakens the male hunter within me.

We're enjoying dinner at Bleu after fighting through paparazzi both outside my residence and in front of the restaurant. Nora is certainly doing an excellent job of keeping us in the media's line of sight. I knew agreeing to become Davina's fiancé would increase my star status, but I had no idea that it would be this chaotic. Yes, I'm a Grammy-winning gospel artist, but I'm not as popular as Davina. I've been in the industry for almost ten years and have released five albums, but few people outside of the Christian community know who I am. Davina, on the other hand, came into the industry less than four years ago and was an instant household name. People who don't normally listen to church music know her songs. She's like the female version of Lecrae or Kirk Franklin, except she sings, raps, and writes her own music. That's what makes her ministry so awesome; she's a triple threat. To be honest, I wish I was as talented and innovative as Davina, but my gifting is solely singing and I'm a firm believer of the phrase, "staying in my own lane."

Our conversation during dinner is a bit stale, so I try to liven it up a bit with industry talk. "Are you nervous about your album release?"

Davina puts down her salad fork and looks up at me vulnerably. "I'd be lying if I said I wasn't. I believed my first album, *Divinity*, was good, but it turned out to be so much bigger than I imagined. I'm still a bit overwhelmed by its success. I feel blessed, but I also feel . . . pressured. There's so much anticipation and high expectations with *The Second Coming*. I don't want to let anyone down, especially God and myself. Have you ever felt that way?"

I nod. "Of course. Fans are so fickle and the music industry is dog-eat-dog. You basically have to fight for everything you get unless you're somebody's powerful child or protégé."

She exhales loudly, seeming relieved by my comments. "Exactly. That's why this whole rumor has got me bummed out. I've worked so hard, and now one stupid lie is ruining everything."

She is wearing a troubled look on her face, and I can't help myself from wanting to be her knight in shining armor. "Davina, I know it's a messed up situation, but it will all work out in the end," I say. "I've seen plenty of scandals in this arena, and good people always find their way through it. You just have to trust God."

She grimaces. "Where was trusting God when they offered me their white lie solution?"

I feel a stab of spiritual conviction. The label's solution isn't perfect, but it's working. Since the news of our engagement, the sales on my last album have tripled. Yet, as much as I'm enjoying the perks, my conscious keeps reminding me that there's always a consequence to sin. I'm just hoping that God's mercy will soften my fall.

"I'm guilty too, Davina, but thank God for grace because we'll both need it after we find our way out of this . . . predicament," I say. "Let's talk about something else. Since I met you, I've been dying to ask you have you always wanted to sing and rap or was it some sort of hidden talent that you stumbled upon."

She offers me half of a smile. "I've always wanted to sing, but I didn't plan for the rapping. I mean, I'm a poet and a songwriter, so somehow the two mixed one day and I wrote my first rhyme. I just played with it for a while for fun, like a hobby or something. But when I was trying to get a record deal and they asked me what set me apart from other gospel singers, without thinking, I blurted out that I could rap too. I did a demo which ended up becoming my first single—'Love Letters'—and instead of having another artist do a cameo appearance for the rap, I did it. The execs loved it, and the rest, as they say, was history."

I'm inspired by her, and I want to tell her so, but at the same time, I don't want to look like a groupie. So I say, "That's a great story. I wish I could do more with my music."

She tilts her head to the left and looks at me as if confused. "What are you talking about? Your music is wonderful. You're already doing great things with it."

I lean in closer, desiring to share with her my innermost thoughts. "Yeah, but you've crossed over into mainstream. Your ministry is so much broader than mine. I wish I could influence as many people as you do."

She straightens her head then shakes it as if she isn't buying anything I'm selling. "Kenny, you know this isn't about me or you or even crossing over. This is about God having a plan for each of us. He decides where our ministries should go and who they should reach. I'm grateful for the distance He's given me, but it doesn't negate the power of Gospel music that is still maintained in the Christian community. Those who need your music are getting it, and each one of those people is precious in God's eyes."

I sit back in my chair and ponder her words. As much as I would like to see my work have a greater reach, I am thankful for the impact it's having closer to home. "I never thought about it like that. I guess I needed to hear that. Thanks."

"Well, what do we have here? I guess the recent rumors are true. You two are really an item."

I look up and see that our much needed conversation is being interrupted by Jill Sweet of *The Juice by Jill*, a popular celebrity blog site. In addition to being an incredibly nosey individual, Jill is also one of the many women who have thrown themselves at me and been rejected. She's attractive and successful in her own right, but I can't trust anyone who finds satisfaction in digging up dirt on others and embarrassing them just because it leads to increased website views. I wonder if she is over our brief yet tragic courtship. It's only been a few months since I told her to lose my number, so there's a chance that she might still be a bit sour about the entire ordeal. In my defense, I wasn't trying to be mean; I just didn't want to lead her on and the constant text messages were ridiculously annoying.

"Can I help you?" Davina asks Jill, making it obvious that she has no clue who the wannabe famous blogger is.

Jill frowns and I want to burst into laughter because I'm certain she perceives Davina's question as a deliberate snub. Instead, I control myself and intervene to ease an already uncomfortable situation. "Davina, this is Jill Sweet. She's a celebrity blogger. Have you ever heard of *The Juice with Jill*?"

Davina's eyes divert to the ceiling as if she is trying to remember, then returns to make contact with mine. "I can't say that I have, but honestly, I don't follow any blogs. I know they're supposed to be the newest news source, but I prefer my news the old fashioned way—the newspaper and six o'clock news." Davina drapes the words with her sweet, Southern accent, making them sound innocent, but a hint of iciness is there and I hear it. I guess Jill does too.

Jill laughs condescendingly. "By the time the newspaper comes out or the six o'clock news comes on, my blog has already reported the story and moved on to the next story. Your preference of the news is slow, dated, and irrelevant."

I probably should interrupt their showdown, but I'm amused and choose to let it continue.

Davina glances at Jill then shrugs. "You're probably right, but with bloggers and other online sites reporting the news so fast, there really isn't much time for research and validation of the story. I find it difficult to believe what's being said when there's a dozen different versions of the story all breaking at the same time. By the time the story ends up in the paper, the news has been properly verified. I'm not trying to undermine your blog, I'm sure it's a great news source, I just feel more at peace with more credible outlets."

Jill's eyes narrow. "Are you trying to say that the outlets that reported that you're a lesbian weren't credible?"

I think Davina's going to lose it, but she remains calm and offers Jill a patronizing smile. "That's exactly what I'm saying. How could that be true when I'm sitting here having dinner with my very manly fiancé?" Davina leans over and kisses me on the cheek, leaving traces of her salmon pink lipstick and an infuriated Jill behind.

Jill chokes on her own saliva. I lift up my untouched glass of water, offering it to her, but she waves it away.

Catching her breath, she says, "I don't know, and that's certainly something I plan to figure out. Three months ago you two weren't dating, but now you're engaged, and conveniently after you've been accused of batting for the other team. Smells fishy to me."

Davina smirks. "No, that's just my lobster bisque. It was a pleasure meeting you, Jan, but if you don't mind, my honey and I would like to finish our meal in private."

Saved or unsaved, every man loves a chick fight, but since I realize there are members of the media lurking—not to mention Jill being one of them—I pray Jill will put her claws away and leave our table quietly. I hold my breath as the two women shoot daggers at each other with their eyes. Just as I feel like I'm about to lose consciousness, Jill backs down. "Fine. And it's Jill," she says, tersely. "Just know that I will find out the truth, and when I do, I'll be sure to let the whole world know."

Jill walks away and I instantly feel relieved. "What was that?" I ask Davina.

Davina shakes her head as if she is shaking off the experience. "My spirit didn't agree with her. There's something really shady about her. You know how you meet someone and everything in you feels bad and yucky?"

I'm amazed that she is able to pick up on Jill's negative vibes. "It's called discernment."

"Yes, discernment. I discerned that Jill Sweet is sour, not sweet. Am I right?"

I laugh. "You're right. She's never done anything too bad—that I know of—but I always feel turned off anytime I'm around her."

Davina looks at me with widened eyes. "Is she an ex?"

I shift in my seat. "Why would you say that?"

"The way she looked at me almost as if I was taking something that belonged to her."

I clear my throat. How do you explain to a woman that you like but aren't really with that you've spent time with another woman that she dislikes without sounding like a player? "I wouldn't call her an ex. We went out on a few dates, but nothing ever came of it."

Davina purses her lips. I can tell that I've just lost a few cool points because I dated Jill. "Maybe not for you, but she definitely is territorial when it comes to you. I thought I was going to have to reach back into my backslider days and pull out a knuckle sandwich with her name on it."

I chuckle. I'm glad she has a good sense of humor. "You're crazy. But that would have been a sight to see."

She balls her right hand into a fist and cups it with her left hand. "Don't sleep on church girls. You know we used to fight in the ladies' bathroom after Sunday school."

I laugh then look around inconspicuously to make sure we're not causing a scene. "I'm not having this conversation with you. Just finish eating your food so we can get out of this restaurant before you turn the whole place out and cost both of us our recording contracts."

Can I Get Some Love On the Radio?

Davina

Dinner with Kenny was surprisingly enjoyable, and two days later, I find myself thinking about him as I ride in a limousine with Rick on our way to a popular radio station. I am scheduled to do an interview during their morning show to promote my upcoming album. I am relieved to be finally getting back to work, focusing my efforts on my new release instead of foolish gossip, yet the silver lining is that I'm almost certain I've gained a new ally inside the industry. Despite his too cool demeanor, Kenny Kauffman is actually a decent guy with a heart of a servant. It should seem as a given that a Christian artist would be all about service, but I've found on many occasions that this is not the norm. Quite possibly, people come into the business wanting to be a servant, but somewhere along the way, the lights and fame bring forth narcissism and self-centeredness. Religious artist, just like secular artists, can easily become caught up in the hype and lose sight of the real reason we do what we do. But

Kenny is still grounded and it's inspiring to see his dedication after a decade in music.

"Are you nervous?" Rick asks me, pulling me away from my thoughts about Kenny.

It takes me a second to shift focus and consider how I feel about the radio interview. I've done tons of media, so I'm really not worried about doing another interview. "Not really. It's all pretty much the same thing every time."

He looks unconvinced. "I think this time will be different."

I apply a layer of lip gloss. Even though it's a radio interview, I still need to look fabulous. Chapped lips are never a good look, and first impressions go a long way. "What makes you say that?"

"This time you're engaged to Kenny Kauffman. This time there are rumors about your sexual preference."

I twist the cap to the lip gloss closed and throw the tube into my purse aggressively. "That's the part that really gets under my skin. If I were a male artist who was speculated to be gay, no one would bat an eye. How many Gospel artists who are men have been rumored to be gay or even caught cheating on their wives and their records continue to sell. But one inkling of gossip that has absolutely no truth to it spreads about me—a woman—and I'm instantly ostracized. If it weren't for this, this *thing* I supposedly have going on with Kenny, I'd probably be kicked out of the church."

Rick offers me a round of applause. " . . . And the Academy Award goes to Davina for her role in *God, Why Me?* Kill the dramatics, cousin. Every industry has its rules, expectations, and biases. If you want to be in this business, you'll just have to suck some stuff up."

I shake my head in disgust. "Sometimes I wonder about you."

"Wonder what?"

"Whose side are you really on?"

"Your side, of course."

I roll my eyes. "It's not about my side or even the industry's side. It's about the side of good or the side of evil. You can't serve two masters, Rick."

Rick smirks. "Neither can you, the soon-to-be Mrs. Kauffman."

I wince at the dig. "Touché."

I look out the window and see that we've made it to the radio station. Rick also notices and begins to adjust his tie, a habit he always does when he's mentally preparing himself to walk into a business situation. Once he seems satisfied, he sighs and looks over at me. "Davina, we all make mistakes and we all make compromises from time to time when it comes to survival or something we really want. But let's not focus on the details right now. Right now, we have a radio interview to do. You ready?"

I am waiting with Rick in the radio station's lobby to be called back for my interview when the entrance door opens and Kenny walks in with Nora. They don't seem surprised to see me, but I'm shocked at their arrival.

"What are you doing here?" I ask Kenny as they make their approach.

He looks from me to Rick to Nora, then back to me. "You don't know?"

I twist my lips and glance over at Rick who is as cool as the other side of the pillow. I quickly realize that he knew they were coming and chose not to tell me.

"Obviously not," Kenny answers for me.

"We understand this is supposed to be your interview, but the label thought it would be beneficial to bring Kenny in on it. The public will want to hear firsthand from the two of you about your relationship," Nora says.

In frustration, I throw my hand up in the air. "This is crazy. I'm trying to promote my album and you want to turn my interview into a circus?"

"It won't be a circus. You have to trust me," Nora says calmly. "You'll still go in there and have your interview, promote your album, and whatever else you intend to do. But at a certain point in the show, Kenny will join you and you'll answer a few questions together. There's enough air time for you to do it all. I promise."

Nora just doesn't get it, and neither does my label. I already hate living this lie. The last thing I want to do is spend the time I'm supposed to be using to promote myself to rehash half-truths and play house with Kenny. I peer back over at Rick who is once again giving me the do-what-you-have-to-do look that he is now becoming famous for. I huff in irritation and step away from all of them. I want to put my foot down, but at that moment, the studio door opens and an assistant calls for me. It's show time, whether I like it or not.

"So, your new album drops July 1st and it's called *The Second Coming*. Davina, talk to us about the album. What can fans expect from this new release?"

My interview during the Mitch Davis Morning Show is going better than I thought. So far Mitch, a comedian turned radio show host, and his morning show crew have been respectful and supportive on the air. I'm relieved that they have chosen to focus on the music instead of the drama, and I show my appreciation by smiling at Mitch before answering his question.

"I put my heart into this album just as I did with the last album, so fans can expect music that is authentic and transparent. I really wanted to go hard on the topic of preparing ourselves for what happens after this life, so that's where the title comes from. It's my second album, but there is a second coming of

Christ and I hope that we're all ready when that day comes. Sometimes, we get so caught up in our daily lives and concerns that we don't spiritually prepare ourselves for the next thing—and not even just eternity, but even for what God has next for us in this life. My first album, *Divinity*, was a blessing for me, but at a certain point, I had to start preparing for my second album. I couldn't just stay stuck, reveling in the success of the first album; I had to move forward and begin considering and planning for what was coming. In that same respect, *The Second Coming* is filled with songs about perseverance, preparation, and progression."

"I like that; that's deep. We're going to play your first single from the new album, a song called 'So What?' But before we play it, tell us a little about this track."

"Sure. I wrote 'So What?' because I kept seeing people around me letting little issues take over their lives. In the full spectrum of life, that person who just cut you off in traffic or the rude cashier at the grocery store are miniscule obstacles. There are much bigger issues at hand. What if when something minor occurred in our daily lives, we just shook it off and said, 'So what?' And that's the chorus: '*So what? I don't focus on those little things. So what? Won't let it rob me of my energy. So what? I'm moving forward, you don't bother me. So what? So what?*'"

"And there you have it. If you're just tuning in, we have the lovely Davina Lacey in the building and here's the first hit single off her new album, 'So What?'"

As soon as the track starts to play, Kenny is led into the room and given a seat next to me. I try not to make eye contact with him as they set him up with earphones and a mic. As much as I like Kenny, I really hate that he's infringing upon my radio interview, and even more so, I hate that with him being here, I'll have to tell more lies about our faux relationship.

I guess Kenny senses that I am still resistant because he comfortingly pats me on my knee. I make eye contact with him and he gazes back at me. It feels as if he is telepathically trying to communicate with me, but I don't read minds, so I am forced to assume that he is thinking that he just wants me to be cool and to go with the flow. I exhale and give in to the situation. But honestly, it's not like I really have a choice. *Do I?*

"We are back with the Mitch Davis Morning Show. You just heard the hit single 'So What?' by Davina, and she is here in the studio this morning. I'm telling y'all, she is a beautiful, talented, and sweet woman, and it's a pleasure having her with us today."

I blush. "Thanks, Mitch. I appreciate all of the love you guys are showing me."

"So, we've got a surprise for our listening audience. For those who don't know, recently Davina became engaged to another Grammy-winning gospel artist, Kenny Kauffman. Kenny is also in the studio with us today and we are excited about finding out about the wedding plans. I mean, this engagement was a shock to us all because we didn't know the two of you were even an item. So Kenny, first of all, thanks for coming on the show. We've had you on a few times in the past and we always love having you with us."

"Thanks a lot, Mitch. It's my pleasure."

"Now, Kenny, tell us about how you met Davina and why we all are just finding out about your relationship."

I look at Kenny, wondering what tricks he is going to pull out of his hat. In our time with Nora, we'd perfected our lie about the engagement, but hadn't spent much time discussing how we met. Thinking back on it, I realize how unprepared we are by not having covered all of the basics of our fictionalized relationship, but there's no time to do a group huddle about the matter now. Mitch Davis has put the question out there and the entire city of Los Angeles is waiting for an answer.

"Well, Mitch," Kenny starts, "you know Davina and I am on the same record label, so we'd seen each other around here and there at different events and whatnot."

That was sort of true. I had seen Kenny several times before officially meeting him recently.

"The first time I saw her, I was star-struck. I'd heard some of her music and thought she was incredibly talented, but to physically see her and how beautiful of a person she is both inside and out, it was like instant chemistry for me. I had to get to know her. Thankfully, I got the opportunity to meet her through a label-related project we are working on, and the rest is sort of history. We've been together ever since."

Okay, so with the exception of the instant chemistry part, the majority of what Kenny is saying is true. I feel like giving him a high five for answering the question in a simple manner without creating this extravagant lie that I'll have to remember the next time someone asks me, but I contain my enthusiasm and nod at him satisfactorily.

"What about you, Davina? What did you think about Kenny when he first approached you?"

"What did I think about Kenny?" I repeat the question to give myself a chance to come up with something believable. "I thought he was very handsome and charming. I'd also heard his music and was very impressed with his career and his passion for God. I guess you could say that I was sort of surprised that he wanted to take a chance on me," I say sincerely. I'm not lying so I don't feel guilty . . . yet.

"So how long have you two been dating and Kenny, what made you decide to propose?" one of Mitch's morning show DJs named Renny asks.

I quickly look over at Kenny. There's no way that either of us can answer these questions without lying. I am starting to feel hot, and if someone doesn't get me out of this studio soon, I'll be sweating bullets.

Kenny keeps his eyes on the DJs, not seeming the least bit concerned about their line of questioning. "We first met about a year ago," Kenny says.

The first time I saw you was about a year ago, but we didn't really meet until several days ago. Half-truths, Kenny.

"And I proposed because the timing was right," Kenny continues. "I needed to make a move that was going to change the both of our lives for the better, so I did."

Good one, Kenny.

"Did your public engagement have anything to do with the rumors that were floating around questioning Davina's sexuality?"

I knew it was coming.

"That's all it was—a rumor," Kenny answers without hesitation. "As a couple, we've decided not to let some fabricated story get in the way of our careers, so we really aren't answering questions about it except to say that it's not true, we don't know where the idea came from, and anyone who is spreading such falsehoods should stop it immediately."

Good save, Kenny. I smile at him, feeling as if my knight in shining armor has rescued me from on-air embarrassment.

"I can respect that, brother," Mitch says. "Our phone lines are blowing up with callers who want to talk to you two, so I think we have time to take about two or three calls before the break." Mitch presses a switchboard button and says, "You're on the Mitch Davis Morning Show. Who am I speaking to?"

"This is Johnny B."

"Where are you calling from, Johnny?"

"I'm calling from Pasadena."

"Well you know, Johnny, we have Davina and Kenny with us this morning. Do you have anything you want to say to them?"

"Yeah. I love y'all and I'm so happy to hear that y'all about to get married. It's like the dream team. Both of you make that hot gospel music. And Kenny, you better treat Davina right or I might have to come take her from you."

Everyone in the studio laughs.

"Looks like you might have some competition, Kenny," Renny says.

Kenny chuckles. "I see that. Thanks, Johnny, for supporting us and don't worry, brother. I'm going to do what it takes to keep my lady happy."

"Okay, okay," Renny says.

"I hear that, Kenny," Mitch says, tapping on the switchboard. "Let's take another call. You're on the line with the Mitch Davis Morning Show. Who am I speaking to, and where are you calling from?"

"This is Lisa from Inglewood. I just wanted to say to Davina that I love your music and can't wait to get your new album. The last one really helped me through some hard times, so I know this album is going to be a blessing, too. And girl, don't even worry about that devil trying to stop your success with those lies about you being gay. I knew it wasn't true. And see how God blessed you right after that with a good looking and successful fiancé. Rebuke that devil and keep doing your thing!"

I don't know how to respond to Lisa's candid words, so I simply say, "Thanks, Lisa. I hope you continue to be blessed by the music."

Mitch works the switchboard again. "Okay, we're going to take one more call. You're on the line with the Mitch Davis Morning Show. Tell us your name and where you're calling from."

"Hello Mitch. This is Jill Sweet from the Juice with Jill. I'm out here in Baldwin Hills."

My stomach turns. Jill is calling the studio to talk to us? After the little scene at the restaurant a few days ago, I'm sure that her call isn't to wish us well.

"Hey Jill. It's always good to hear from you," Mitch says.

"Likewise. I was listening in on your interview, and I hate to be the one to tell you, but I think these two are a fraud. My instinct and sources are telling me that Davina is still in the closet and this proposal has publicity stunt written all over it."

Mitch's eyes widen in surprise and he instantly looks over at Kenny at me for our reaction. We glance at each other and shrug as if we're completely innocent. "Whoa, Jill! Those are some mighty big accusations," he says, seemingly in an attempt to manage the situation.

"They are, but I know for a fact that Kenny couldn't have been dating Davina for the past year because he was dating me only a few months ago," Jill says with a smug tone of voice.

Renny squeals and says, "Oh my goodness! I can't believe my ears! Did Jill just call in to the show and put Kenny Kauffman on blast? Kenny, my friend. Tell me this isn't true."

Kenny licks his lips then clears his throat. Before responding, he reaches under the table and grabs my hand. I'm glad he does it because my anxiety level is through the roof. If he wasn't here to speak for me, I'd probably run out of the room in tears. I've never been good with public confrontation.

"I did go out on a few dates with Jill, but it was never anything serious," Kenny says calmly. "At that time, Davina and I were not exclusive. We were seeing each other, but because of our busy careers, we couldn't commit to the relationship. I really don't know what kind of game Jill is playing, but I think it's pretty disrespectful to call the show and come at me and my fiancé in this manner. It appears that she might be the one pulling a publicity stunt. Mitch, I appreciate the love that your team has shown us this morning, and I hope the listening audience checks out Davina's new album. I've heard most of the tracks and it's a powerful album. Her fans won't be disappointed."

Mitch nods at Kenny and smiles. I find myself smiling too.

"Well, there you have it folks," Mitch says, turning the switchboard off in the process. "You heard it here. Kenny Kauffman backs up his woman 100 percent. That's love, y'all. We're going to break, but when we come back, we'll have our inspirational minute with Dr. Yolanda Morrow."

How Deep is Your Love
...or Hate?

Kenny

I act nonchalant around Davina and the Mitch Morning Show staff, but inside I am fuming. I can't believe Jill's shenanigans. I knew the lady was a bit off in the head, but now I am convinced that she is certifiably crazy. What is she trying to prove? Is she really that desperate? Is she truly that hurt by the fact that we didn't work out that she would go so far as to attack me and Davina on nationally syndicated radio?

For three days following the radio incident, the situation replays over and over in my head. Everything I try to do to get my mind off the matter doesn't do the job. Working out at the gym, shooting hoops with the fellas, recording a new song in the studio, even hanging out with Davina isn't enough to silence the uneasiness about Jill's behavior. Unable to bear much more of the torture, I find myself going to God in prayer for peace. I know prayer should have been my first course of action, but like most people, I think I can handle issues that I cannot, and often wait until I've exhausted every other route before I take my problems to the throne.

"Why can't I shake these thoughts, God? Help me to forgive Jill like you've forgiven me. I've done so much worse," I pray.

The memory of seeing Jill at the restaurant flashes through my mind. I instantly tense up.

"Free me from this bondage. I don't want to carry this."

I hear Jill's voice saying hurtful things about me over the radio. About Davina.

"God, I know we're wrong for our lies, but don't allow Jill to hurt Davina."

Because of Jill's accusations on the radio, a new wave of negative media has popped up about Davina's sexuality and whether or not our relationship is real. Thankfully, most of our fans seem to be siding with us, unwilling to believe that a gossip blogger like Jill could be telling the truth. Although Jill is an attractive woman, people don't think I would ever date someone like her. Based on the tweets and social media comments, Davina is a perfect match for me, and Jill is simply a hater. Nora has kept Davina and I updated on the newest hashtags about us: #JillTakeASeat and #TeamKevina. I can't believe we've been given a merged couples' name.

I laugh at the thought of the social media hashtag directed at Jill Sweet. It feels good to laugh at the matter rather than being frustrated. I really want to let it go, but for some reason, I feel a strong urge to call Jill and confront her about her behavior. I get up off my knees—my favorite prayer position—and pick my cell phone up from my nightstand. Without delay, I scroll through my contacts for Jill's number and give her a call.

"Hey, loverboy," she answers. "It took you long enough to call."

"You expected me to call you after that stunt you pulled the other day?" I say, incensed.

She giggles. "Of course. Calm down. There's no need to get all stressed out about it."

I can't believe that she thinks this game she's playing is cute of funny. Her lack of a conscious about it makes me dislike her even more. "Jill, what you're doing is not cool. What's the deal with you?"

She sighs. "The deal is that I want you to kick Miss Gospel Princess to the curb."

This woman must have lost her mind. Who told her that she has any say in who I'm with? "Why? It's not like you and I are ever going to be together," I say, intentionally trying to cut her down.

"Hmm. Maybe that's true. We aren't together and may never be, but you won't be with Davina either. I honestly don't see what you see in her. She's a *les-bi-an*," Jill says, emphasizing the word, "which means she doesn't like men. And furthermore, she's not even that great of a singer."

I shake my head in disgust. "You're delusional and I don't have time for this. Just stop, okay?"

"Stop what?"

"Stop writing a bunch of nonsense on your blog, accusing Davina of all sorts of dumb stuff. She's not a *les-bi-an*, and we are together whether you like it or not. You're just going to have to learn to live with it."

"No, you're going to have to learn how to be a better liar. I know that this engagement isn't real and I won't stop until I dig up the truth," Jill says, sounding irritated. "I don't know why you're putting your own career in jeopardy to help her, but I will find out the truth. It's my job, and despite whatever we used to have, I feel the public needs to know that they are being deceived by two so-called Christians. Isn't lying a sin?"

"Isn't gossiping a sin?" I say mockingly.

"Whatever, Kenny. I'm warning you. If you don't give up this little show you and Davina are acting out, I will shut it down."

"Why is this so important to you?" I ask, completely flustered.

"I could ask you the same question."

"What are you trying to prove?"

"That I'm right."

If I weren't a child of God, I would be in route to her house to snatch her up, but I know I can't handle my problems with violence. Plus, assaulting Jill would kill my career faster than anything Jill could write about me in her stupid blog. Instead, I grit my teeth and say, "Mind your business and have a blessed day, Jill."

I hang up the phone and toss it across the room in anger. Luckily, I have an excellent phone case and it keeps the phone from breaking when it crashes to the floor seconds later. Jill is insane and determined. Those are two qualities you don't want to see working at the same time because it leads to guaranteed chaos. I really like Davina; I truly care for her to the point that I may have to end this engagement with her simply to protect her from Jill. People like Jill never give up. They feel compelled to prove their point. I know she's not calling my bluff— she won't stop until she proves that she is right. Of course, she's not right about Davina's sexuality, but she's dead on about the manufactured engagement. This is a huge mess. I should have known that lying was going to lead us to a worse place than we were when we began.

I pace the floor of my living room several times, trying to come up with a plan. No matter how I twist and turn the matter, I realize that there is no way Davina and I can continue the label's scheme and not end up with our careers destroyed. The best option is that we call the engagement off. At least that way we can part ways with our dignity and careers still intact. I sigh deeply and resolve the issue within. I have to tell Davina and the label that it's over. I'm backing out.

Let's Get Married

Davina

I **don't know how I ended up** back in the same boardroom with the same players exactly two weeks after the first time we did this dance, but somehow, I find myself seated once again between Rick and Kenny, waiting for the label exes to ask me something else crazy like sacrifice my first born child. The déjà vu feeling is overwhelming, and I can't help but poke Rick in his side in an attempt to get him to reassure me that this meeting is purely a formality. When he doesn't respond—not even a wince or wink—I know trouble is brewing. I suck in my breath.

"How's our favorite couple doing?" Mr. Bradley asks. He is smiling, but I don't believe that he is happy. I've seen plenty of fake smiles and he is definitely wearing one.

"That's what I need to talk to you all about," Kenny says before I can begin to come up with a response to the cryptic question.

I glance over at Kenny who makes direct eye contact with me then looks away. The last couple of days, he's been distant. He hasn't spent any time with me or called me. I thought we were building a friendship, but maybe I was wrong.

"People are becoming suspicious of our relationship. I'm worried that this whole thing is going to blow up in our faces," he says.

"Exactly," Mr. Bradley says. "We need to make an immediate change."

Kenny exhales as if he feels relieved. I want to have the same feeling, but I'm still waiting for the other shoe to drop.

"Thank God," Kenny whispers.

Although his acknowledgement of God was probably not intended as a put down to me, it stings that he wants to be rid of me. *Why the sudden change?*

Mr. Bradley's smile vanishes. "It's time for you two to get married."

"What?" Kenny and I say in unison.

He leans back in his chair. "Well, you don't have to technically get married, but you need to start planning a wedding as if you're really engaged. People are only suspicious because outside of a few dates and an expensive ring, they don't see the makings of a wedding. You two have to play the role. Davina, go out and start shopping for dresses. Kenny, put a deposit down on a banquet hall or reserve a church. Give the people what they want—a wedding."

Kenny and I look at each other, and for the first time in days, it seems as if we are back on the same page. From the dull look in his eyes, I can tell he is thinking what I'm thinking—Mr. Bradley is cuckoo!

I realize that I should have said no to the foolishness two weeks ago, but since I had a short lapse in judgment, it's time that I finally do the right thing. "Okay, lying about being engaged is one thing, but planning a wedding to a guy I'm not in love with is completely out of the question. No offense, Kenny."

"None taken," Kenny says. "She's right. This is going way too far."

"You really don't have any other options," Ms. Thompson interjects. "If you two break-up now, it will only confirm that the relationship wasn't real in the first place."

"It wasn't," I say with conviction.

Mr. Bradley leans in to the table. "But do you want your fans to know that? Do you want your fans to know that you've been deceiving them for the past two weeks for the sake of saving your career?"

"It was *your* idea," I say then immediately regret my words. Not that it wasn't their idea, but I know I'm not taking responsibility for going along with it no matter whose idea it was. My rebuttal sounds like that of an entitled child.

Mr. Bradley lets out a weary sigh. Patience is most likely not his best trait. "But it's *your* career. If you end this now, your album will probably flop. People will be so consumed by the rumors and speculation, they won't care that *The Second Coming* is one of the best gospel albums to ever hit the market. I would love to tell you that talent alone will take you to the top, but everyone in this business knows that talent is never enough. More than talent, you have to be liked, better yet, loved. The fans love Kenny and Davina, or what is it, Kevina? As a couple, you two could move gospel music into the mainstream like never before. Just imagine it. It could be amazing."

I look at Rick who is as usual giving me that do-what-you-have-to-do look. I don't know why I expect anything different. My cousin has sold me out and I let him. I feel trapped like caged bird. *God, have mercy.*

"I don't know, Mr. Bradley. This is not God's way," I say more to myself than him. "And really, what is me buying a wedding dress going to do that telling people we're engaged hasn't already done?"

Mr. Bradley smirks. "Well, let's see. This morning, your wedding date was leaked to the media."

Kenny jumps to his feet. "Our what date?"

Mr. Bradley nods in Nora's direction. "Nora, how's that going?"

She is holding an iPad and turns the screen to face those of us in the room. "The fans are beside themselves. New trending hashtag on Twitter: #KevinaSaveTheDate."

"I can't believe this," Kenny says, now pacing the floor. "Why would you do this to us?"

Ms. Thompson motions for Kenny to take a seat, and after hesitating for a moment, he obliges. "Because this company has invested a lot of money into the both of you. You cannot fail us," she says.

I'm upset, but feel powerless. Deep inside, I want to scream at all of them and throw the biggest fit ever, but it won't change anything. What's done is done. "So when's this so called wedding?" I ask, bitterness in my voice.

"In six weeks. Two weeks after Davina's album releases," Ms. Thompson answers.

I am shocked by the timing. Six weeks is like six days—it's just too soon. No one plans a wedding in six weeks. It's almost as if they want this plan to fall apart. "Why so soon?" I ask, completely confused.

Mr. Bradley leans back again in his chair. "Publicity. Why else?"

There's No Business Like Show Business

Kenny

We have six weeks to put a wedding together, a wedding that probably will never happen. The label's plan has so many holes that it feels like a golf course. Are we expected to call the wedding off at the last minute? What's the point of spending all of this money on wedding details if there won't be an event? The label talks about losing money if we don't follow through with their scheme, but won't all of this hoopla cost just as much? No matter how I try to understand this ordeal, it doesn't seem to add up. The more of a mess the situation becomes, the more I regret getting involved in the first place. I like Davina a lot, I may even be falling in love with her, but there has to be a better way to get close to her than this.

I'm uneasy about the ordeal, but I continue to go along with the label's plan. I ask my pastor who is also a personal friend to allow us to reserve his church for the wedding. Luckily, there is a cancellation for the set wedding day, and he schedules our ceremony immediately. I was sort of hoping that the church would be booked so I could use it as an excuse to push back or even cancel the wedding, but it seems as if God isn't going to let us out of this mess so easily. With no other choice but to move forward, I also book a swanky lounge for our reception. Since I am not expecting us to actually get married, I keep the catering menu simple, asking only for hors d'oeuvres, champagne, and a wedding cake.

Meanwhile, Davina is given the task of sending out invitations to one-hundred of our closest friends and family members. She calls me every day whining about how guilty she feels every time someone RSVPs. Some of the guest will be coming from out-of-town, so she hates the idea that they will make travel plans for a wedding that won't occur. I also feel bad, but what else can we do besides follow through or tell the truth?

The weekend before Davina's album drops, she hosts a listening party at Savor, an upscale restaurant in downtown L.A. Nora arranges for Davina and me to be transported to the event in a limousine. As we travel from my condo to the event's location, I watch Davina closely. She looks amazing, wearing a sparkly black top and wide-legged black pants. Her hair is styled in a curly up-do, drawing attention to her high cheek bones and big, round eyes. I can tell than she is jittery because she keeps rubbing her hands over her pants and biting her lower lip. As much as I'm not ready to get married to anyone, if I were, she would be the perfect candidate.

"It's going to be great," I say to her. "You look wonderful, and everyone is going to love the album. Don't look so worried."

She lets out a nervous giggle. "Is it that obvious?"

I nod. "Yeah."

"Thanks." She exhales and smiles. "Thanks for coming with me tonight. I know we're supposed to be this couple and all, but you could have just met me there."

"No, I couldn't. Nora would have flipped out if we'd shown up separately."

"Yeah, you're right about that."

I reach out and grab her hand. "But I'm glad I can support you tonight. You deserve this."

She looks at me skeptically. "Do I? Lately, I haven't felt much deserving of anything. Kenny, this whole ordeal is killing me."

I squeeze her hand. "Me, too. But it will be over soon. Your album comes out on Tuesday, and after that, we will find a way to call it off. But despite all of the lies, you do deserve the success of this album. You worked really hard to make this music way before any of this engagement stuff. Know that none of this mess we're in changes your heart or what you put into this album. Okay?"

"Okay."

When our limo pulls up to the curb in front of Savor, there is a decent sized crowd surrounding a red carpet, awaiting the guest of honor. Photographers incessantly snap pictures as Davina and I exit the vehicle. She holds my hand with her left hand and waves at the crowd with her right as we make our way toward the restaurant's front door. Before we move indoors, she breaks away from me for a minute to sign a few autographs before giving the crowd a last wave and walking into the building.

Inside, the "by invite only" partygoers offer Davina a standing ovation the moment we enter and she is announced to the room. Songs from her new album are blaring from the overhead speakers and the guests seem to be enjoying it. I move away from her, allowing her to greet her attendees and make her rounds.

I head to the bar and order a ginger ale before focusing my attention on the various people who approach Davina. The label executives move close to her, wearing smug expressions as if her success is theirs. I hate the idea that they think they've created the success that Davina has come to be. Yes, they played their roles, but ultimately it is God who gave her the favor, talent, and increase.

I notice that after a minute or two of small talk, they begin to search the crowd. They're looking for me, making sure their plan is going the exact way they envisioned. When they spot me leaning against the bar, they wave and gesture for me to join them. I nod and smile politely, but have no intentions of making my way over to them.

That is until Jill Sweet plants herself next to me at the bar.

"Great party. Too bad her success won't last," Jill says as she leans toward me and somewhat whispers in my ear.

I jerk back, not wanting to be close to her and definitely not wanting to feel her hot breath on my skin. "What are you doing here? I know Davina didn't invite you."

"I have my ways," she said coolly. "Besides, I couldn't miss Davina's big day, especially when I'm working so hard to take it all away from her."

"If you have a problem with me, take it up with me and leave Davina out of it." I snarl.

She flips her hair. Everything about her is so fake that I'm sure her hair is too. "I don't have a problem with you or Davina. I just have a duty to expose the truth, especially when so-called Christians are behaving badly."

"So you have a problem with Christians?"

She twists her lips. "I have a problem with self-righteous people who judge everyone and think they're the only ones God loves."

I let out a sarcastic laugh. "That's funny because your behavior is extremely self-righteous and you're the biggest judge of them all. I'm so tired of people trying to slap Christian's hands for being judgmental, but when anyone else in the world has a problem with something, it's okay for that person to speak his or her mind. Yes, at times we all, including Christians, have been a bit overly critical of others, but that doesn't make me a bad person for being honest with my fellow brother or sister when I see them headed in the wrong direction. It actually shows my love for others when I'm not afraid to hold those I care about accountable for their actions. You have to stand for something or you'll end up falling for anything. Obviously, you subscribe to the latter."

Jill looks stunned by my rebuttal and opens her mouth, yet nothing comes out. I take it as my window of opportunity to get away from her and say, "If you'll excuse me, my date is waiting for me."

I hadn't planned to join Davina and the label executives, but I grab my soda from the bar and head over to the center of the party where my fiancée greets me with a sincere smile.

I Give Myself Away

Davina

The album releases at #1 on the Billboard charts in Top Gospel Albums and #7 on the Billboard 200. The music critics instantly begin posting reviews, highly praising the overall album, calling it refreshing, inspiring, hard-hitting, and Grammy nomination worthy. I am ecstatic. Two months ago, I feared my album would be irredeemably tainted by the vicious rumors about me, yet now I am basking in the glow of a job well done. Unfortunately, I still feel awful about the lies I've told to cover my own butt, and the fact that Kenny and I are technically still engaged. The reality is this whole façade has got to end.

It's a week and a half before the wedding, and I am at a bridal shop in Beverly Hills, trying on designer wedding gowns. Personally, I would never buy a $20,000 dress, but the label is paying for it, so I may as well enjoy splurging. Since none of my family or friends know what's going on with this whole wedding sham and most of them live on the east coast, I am actually at a boutique wedding shop with Nora of all people. If I were really getting married, I would want my people close to me right now, but since I'm a liar-liar-pants-on-fire, I want everyone who loves me to stay far away—with the exception of Cousin Rick who got me into this mess to begin with.

As I try on each of the five dresses that have been hand-picked for my body shape and budget, I model them for Nora who gives the dresses a thumbs up or thumbs down. By the time I get to the final dress, she has only given her stamp of approval on two of the dresses. One is a strapless gown with a white beaded bodice and a puffy, Cinderella looking skirt. The other—which I currently have on—is a somewhat form-fitting dress with a halter style top and a lengthy train. I gaze at myself in the mirror, relishing the beauty of the fine gown. I've never cared much about whether or not I would get married, but seeing myself in such an exquisite wedding dress makes me want to get hitched, if just simply to look this stunning for an entire day.

"I like this one," I say to Nora, looking at her through the mirror's reflection.

"Good. That's one more thing to check off our list." She starts fooling with her cellphone, probably tweeting out that I just found a wedding dress. Nora is so focused, which I can appreciate because she reminds me of myself. But when someone is focused on keeping me in my own private hell, it's hard to appreciate their diligence.

"Why are you doing this?" I ask her, causing her to briefly look away from her phone.

"Doing what?"

I gently sit down in the cushioned white chair next to her, trying not to wrinkle the dress. "This," I say. "This whole thing with the label. I mean, I know it's your job, but do you really like helping us deceive the world? Are you even sleeping at night after all of the lies we've told? If you are, please tell me your secret because I can't get more than four or five hours of sleep, and I need a minimum of ten just to function."

Nora lowers the phone and looks over at me. I finally have her complete attention. "Yes, it's my job and I'm good at it. And yes, I can sleep at night. Some of our behaviors have not been the most holy, but we're doing it for a good reason—to make sure good music that this world needs to hear has a chance to survive. I guess that's how I rationalize it to myself. That and the fact that I have a zillion bills that need to be paid."

I nod, relating to the need to keep the bills paid. "I just wish we could have found a better way to save my album, something that didn't require all of this hoopla."

She tilts her head to the right. "This is really bothering you, huh?"

I sigh. "It really is."

"Then why didn't you just say no. You've been in control the entire time. At any point, you could have stopped this plan. You know that, right?"

I shrug. "Yes and no. I could have, but I felt, and still feel, like so much is riding on me going along with it. My career, Kenny's career, possibly the world's view of Gospel music as a whole."

She lets out a grunt. "You're not responsible for other's perceptions about the faith. People are going to either believe in God or they aren't. That's their choice, no matter what they see others do."

It's at that moment that I realize Nora's been working with me for weeks and I know absolutely nothing about her. I don't know where she lives, where she went to school, if she's married, or if she has children. I don't even know if she's a Christian. I just automatically assumed that she was a woman of faith since she agreed to work with me. "Do you believe in God?" I ask her.

She offers me a small smile. "Yes, I do."

"You believe in God, but you're not concerned about two Gospel singers lying to the world for their own selfish reasons?"

"Listen, Davina. I'm not perfect. I've made many mistakes along the way, so I can't look down at you and Kenny or even let this situation change my thoughts about religious artists. Sure, it's wrong, but at some point, you're going to have to make it right."

I lower my eyes to the floor. "I guess that's what I'm afraid of."

"Davina, I'm going to tell you something that I should have told you from the beginning, but I wasn't sure how to do so and still keep things professional."

I look up at her in anticipation. It would be nice to know more about her than just her last name. "I'm listening."

"I'm not telling you this for shock purposes; I just want you to understand why I'm working with you." She sighs then says, "I used to be a lesbian. I lived that lifestyle for over ten years. It's one of the reasons that the label assigned me to help with your situation. They knew that I knew the GLBT community and how to distance someone from appearing as if they are a part of that community. I had to distance myself when I changed my lifestyle. It wasn't easy. The difficulty in your situation wasn't just getting heterosexuals to believe that you weren't a lesbian, it was getting the gay community to believe it as well. That was where the rumor started, and that's where it had to be cut down most."

It takes me a second to process her words. *She used to be a lesbian? This is why she was assigned to help me? She changed?* I have a boatload of questions forming inside my mind, but the one that slips out of my mouth first is, "It started in the gay community?"

She nods. "Yes. I tracked down the original source of the rumor and it was a celebrity blog. The blogger is a 'closet' bisexual. Gay people know she swings both ways, but straight folks are clueless."

I want to know more about her story, but I have this nagging feeling that the source of my nasty rumor isn't as mysterious as I had previously believed. "Would this blogger happen to be Jill Sweet of *The Juice with Jill*?"

Nora looks away for a moment. I can tell that she is contemplating whether or not she should tell me more. The fact that she hesitates is all of the answer I need. It is Jill; I have no doubt about it, but I still await Nora's response to confirm my belief as true. "I was told not to tell you this, but yes. We believe that Jill is the one who started the rumor. All of the evidence that I've found points back to her."

I was tempted to scream, but I didn't want to attract any more attention than already surrounded me. Paparazzi were waiting outside, hoping to get a glance of my selected gown. A scream would be all of the provoking they would need to storm through the door with cameras in hand. "That little . . . I can't believe she would do this to me. I didn't even know her before all of this."

"Well apparently she knew about you and felt the need to hurt you."

"This is so crazy. I should have known she had something to do with it. Thanks for telling me all of this, even though you weren't supposed to. I just don't know why she's so singularly focused on me. . . Do you think she wants me or something?"

Nora chuckles. "I wouldn't worry about that if I were you. I think she's more interested in Kenny than you."

"Sorry, I know that was a stereotypical assumption," I say, feeling a bit embarrassed about my runaway imagination. "I just don't understand why she's so set on bringing me down. If she likes Kenny, I sort of get why she would have an issue with me now that the world thinks we're engaged, but when the initial rumor about my sexuality began, Kenny and I barely knew each other."

Nora shrugs and says, "Maybe you should be asking Kenny about this instead of me."

"I guess you're right," I say, agreeing that Kenny would know much more about Jill than Nora. Resolved to let go of my inquiries about Jill for the moment, curiosity about a different matter resurfaced. "Can I ask you a question . . . about you?"

"Sure. What's up?"

I move a bit closer to her, not wanting to speak too loudly when asking such a personal question. "You said you no longer live that lifestyle. Why did you change? I'm only asking because some people say that they're born gay and can't change."

Nora smiles, which is a relief to me because I didn't want to offend her. "All of us have the capacity to change ourselves and the way we live our lives, some things are just harder to change than others," she says. "For me, I was attracted to women and didn't think I would ever feel the same way about men. The closer my relationship with God became, the more I felt myself struggling with my lifestyle. Honestly, for a long time I believed being gay was something I would always be. But slowly, over time, I began to realize that I did have a choice, but I had to make a commitment to it because my very nature was the opposite of what I knew God was calling me to be. It's sort of like being on a diet. You know you're overweight and you should do something about it, but everything in you wants to keep eating whatever you want because that's what feels good and that's what feels natural. All of the while you know that if you keep eating junk, the consequences could be life threatening. At some point, you have to make a decision which is more important, your life or your desires. And even if you choose your life, you're still going to have to war against your desires every day until a new way of living replaces the old, and that takes time—sometimes years to happen. Choosing my relationship with God over my sexual desires was similar. It wasn't an easy process, but He honored me for my commitment, and over time, my desires changed."

"Wow," I say as I mull over her response. "Most people would have just accepted being gay and not fought so hard to make a change."

She drops her cellphone into her purse. It's the first time I've ever seen her without it in the palm of her hand. I've obviously struck a chord with her, because she continues to school me. "The Bible says that there is a way that seems right to a man, but at the end is death. There are a lot of things that our natural bodies want that are not good for us. There are a lot of things that feel good and look good that really hurt us. We were born in sin and shaped in iniquity. From the day we are born, we are inclined to miss the mark, to miss the higher calling of God. We all have areas of our lives that we have to sacrifice, that we have to put under the subjection of God's will and not our own. I'm not trying to preach to you, because Lord knows that I'm still so far from living in obedience, and I guess helping you and Kenny lie isn't helping me earn any jewels in my heavenly crown. But when they offered me the job, something stirred within me. Yeah, I appreciated the money, but it was more than that. I guess I thought I could help, yet I'm not sure if I did."

Her words hit home for me. Maybe I wasn't struggling with homosexuality, but I still had my flaws and they needed to be submitted to God. "You've helped," I admit. "Not because you plotted and planned with the label to save my album, but because you were so transparent with me just now. We overcome by the word of our testimony. It reminds me why I'm fighting so hard for my career—my ministry. I think I'm going to talk to Kenny and figure out a way to terminate this engagement before the label has us walking down the aisle and exchanging vows against our wills. I became a Gospel artist so that I could spread the good news. Every song that I write is an opportunity to help someone get to know God, and I have to be willing to follow His way, even if it means sacrificing my own will and desires. You have a very powerful testimony. Keep sharing it with others and you'll help a lot of people."

"I will," she says, then looks at me critically. "In the meantime, let's get you out of this expensive dress."

"Oh, yes!" I say then carefully stand and begin to remove the luxurious garment.

For the Record

Kenny

I am at my condo, trying unsuccessfully to write a new song when I hear the doorbell ring. I wasn't expecting anyone and had not buzzed anyone up into the building. I figure it's either one of my neighbors that I've become friendly with, or it's Davina who has carte blanche to come up. I toss the pen and pad I am using on top of my baby grand piano and make my way to the door, not worrying about checking the peephole to see who's there. I swing the door open and see Davina standing on the other side with a sullen expression on her face. Backing away from the door, I allow her to come inside and I begin to wonder why she's here and what has got her in a funk. I pray Jill has not bothered Davina, throwing another of her fiery darts.

"Are you okay?" I ask once she is fully inside my residence and I've closed and locked the door behind her.

"No. No, I'm not," she says, while walking over to the sofa and taking a seat in the spot she seems to claim every time she comes over.

I feel my muscles tense. Over the past several weeks, I've become extremely protective of Davina. She's my friend, and I can't deny my growing affection for her. "What's wrong? What happened? Did Jill try something else?" I ask more anxiously than I meant. For some reason, lately, I haven't been my usual composed self around her.

She sighs and removes her purse strap from her shoulder, placing the designer clutch on the ottoman in front of her. "I found out that Jill is the one who started the rumors about me."

"What? Who told you that?" Although the news is not surprising, it does nothing to relieve my increasing tension.

"Nora," she says. "You know how Nora seems to know everything. She did some research and believes Jill was the original source."

I think about what Davina is telling me. I didn't suspect Jill despite her antics because the timeline doesn't fit. I believe Jill is capable of such slander, but what could have motivated her to spread gossip about Davina almost two months ago? "That doesn't make complete sense," I say. "She didn't even know you then, and we weren't engaged, so I don't know why she would target you."

She shrugs. "That's what I said. I don't get why she would single me out amongst all of the Christian artists out today. Why me of all people?"

I take a seat next to her and think about my past interactions with Jill. I'd only been in her presence about a half a dozen times so it wasn't difficult to mull over what I remembered about her. For a few minutes, Davina and I sat in silence. I imagine that she was doing the same thing I was—trying to figure out the why behind Jill's behavior. Then suddenly, a memory plays clearly in my mind that provides the answer I'm seeking.

"I think I know why," I say while shaking my head in disbelief. "It's because of me. How could I have missed that?"

Davina gives me a comforting pat on the shoulder. "It can't be your fault. We didn't know each other then."

I look up at her, apologetically. "I'm sorry, Davina. I'd completely forgotten."

"Forgotten what?"

I shift my body on the sofa so that I am now facing her. "You remember when I told you that she and I went out on a few dates before I stopped communicating with her, right?"

"Yeah."

"I think it was on the second date, she asked me this weird question. Something like if I could go on a date with any celebrity or artist in the industry, who would I pick? At first, I tried not to answer the question because what woman really wants to hear a man talk about another woman in a positive light unless it's like his mother. But she kept asking, saying she was just curious. I had just been listening to one of your songs earlier that day, so I thought about you and said your name to her. I didn't think it was a big deal, and I definitely didn't think she would pick a fight with you over it. Now that I think about it, it makes complete sense why she doesn't believe that we're together because when I said your name, I didn't say it like we were already an item; I said it like I thought it would be cool to get to know you. I'm really sorry, Davina. How was I supposed to know that she was going to become so jealous of you?"

Davina grimaced then let out a chuckle. "It's okay. It's not your fault. If a guy would have asked me the same question, I probably would have answered it too, not considering why he was asking. I guess Jill must really like you. Oh, yeah, that's another thing. Nora told me that Jill likes both men and women. I don't want to spread gossip or anything, but I think you should know the truth about her since she has her eyes set on you."

Jill being bisexual is surprising, however, as it relates to having a romantic relationship with her, I am unconcerned. "Don't worry about me," I say. "There's nothing that woman can do or say that will ever make me want to go out with her again. Plus, I think I'm interested in someone else."

Davina's eyes grow wider. "Really? Who?"

She can be so naïve at times. It's one of things that I adore about her. "She's a beautiful, famous Gospel singer with a chart topping album," I say.

A smile slowly creeps across her face. "Me?"

I find myself grinning too. "Yeah. You." I lean in and kiss her lightly on the cheek. I would have went for her soft looking lips, but I'm not sure how she feels about me, and I don't want to move too fast.

She looks at me with gentle eyes. "Kenny, this is very flattering. To tell you the truth, I've also come to enjoy being around you, but we can't keep this engagement charade up and we certainly can't get married ten days from now."

I know that she's right, but I don't want what we have to end—not when it was just starting to get good. "Maybe we can," I say with a hint of desperation in my voice. "I mean, we can look at it like an arranged marriage."

She giggles and hits my lightly on my arm. "Kenny, stop playing. You know we can't go through with this. It's not God's way."

The sad part is that I wasn't playing. I like Davina a lot. I feel as if I'm falling for her, but it's obvious that her feelings for me aren't exactly the same. It's understandable. The entire situation was never supposed to get serious. Like Mr. Bradley said, it was all about the publicity. "Yeah, you're right," I say in defeat. "You can't blame me for trying."

Davina grabs my hand, squeezes it, and then lets it go. "I do like you, but if I ever get married, I want it to be the right way with the man that God has for me. Everything we've been doing has been so backwards that I can't tell what's my will and what's His."

I can't argue with her rationale. As much as I hate to lose her, trying to patch together a relationship that started as a lie can't be God's divine plan. If there is a future for us, we have to end the current situation and trust God that He knows how to repair our mess. "So what do we do?" I ask a bit sorrowfully.

She looks away from me as if she can't bear to see the look on my face anymore. "We meet with members of the press and tell the world, on the record, that we've called the wedding off."

Let Go

Davina

I know it's the right thing to do, but publically breaking off my engagement to Kenny is much harder than I imagined. After I leave Kenny's condo, I arrive home to find Rick sitting at my dining room table, waiting for me. Well, he says he was waiting for me, but the fact that he has raided my refrigerator and is eating up my leftover Teriyaki Chicken from last night makes me think he really came over for a free meal.

"You could have asked," I say begrudgingly. It was my intention to have the food for dinner, but by default, I would have to eat something else.

"You could have been home," he says. "I've been calling you for three hours and I've been waiting here for the past two. I got hungry so . . ."

I frown at him, roll my eyes, and begin to rummage through my cabinets and fridge, looking for a suitable alternative. "I've been busy," I say. "What do you want?"

"When I spoke to you this morning, you sounded . . . different. I can tell you're up to something. I felt the need to stop you before you do something that you'll regret."

When I only come up with a box of cereal and half gallon of milk to eat, I huff in frustration. I need to take back my house key from Rick. Showing up without permission is one thing, but eating my dinner is another. "Look, Rick, you're not my father, so chill out. And if you ever come over my house again and start eating up my food without permission, you won't be my cousin anymore."

"Oh, you want some?" he asks, offering me the last few morsels left of the Asian dish.

"Don't be cute, Rick," I scold. "Again, what do you want?"

He scoops one last forkful of food into his mouth, chews, and swallows it before saying, "You're about to pull out of this engagement, aren't you?"

I lean against the granite countertop. "And if I do?"

Wiping his mouth with a paper napkin, he says, "I'm not saying that I expect you to marry Kenny, but if you did, it wouldn't be that terrible. I'm just saying, Kenny is a successful guy and there are a lot of women who would be happy to be in your position. Just think about it."

It burns me up that he still thinks this foolish plan is a good idea. "Okay, let's get a few things straight between you and me," I say. "First, this is my life and you don't have any right trying to tell me who I should be happy to be with. Second, you are not only my manager, but you're my family. I have trusted you to help me make good decision, but it seems that the only thing you even care about these days is success by any means necessary."

He looks at me as if he's confused. "Don't you want to be successful?"

"Of course."

"Then I'm doing my job."

"No, you're not. I could have gotten anyone to be my manager if I was only concerned about being successful without integrity, but that's not who I am, and when I hired you, I didn't think that was who you were either. You used to always preach about doing the right thing. What happened to you? Don't you care about what happens to me in the end? Don't you care about pleasing God anymore?"

His eye widen and for the first time in a long time, I think I have finally gotten through that thick skull of his. He scratches his head then lets out a sigh. "Of course, I care about those things," he says. "I just . . . I just thought . . . I guess I just got caught up. I'm sorry, cousin. I wasn't trying to hurt you. I wanted you to be successful so badly that I let myself get caught up in all of the hype.

"You're right. I haven't been the best manager or cousin lately. I was ready to come over here and talk you into going as far as to marrying a man that you don't love just so that I could be connected to your rise to the top."

Although I am glad that he's finally agreeing with me, I can't help but feel a tad bit guilty that I've made him the scapegoat. "You aren't the only one to blame. I could have said no."

"But I was pretty persuasive."

"I still could have said no." I walk over to the table and sit down across from him "I wanted the success too. I guess we both have some repenting to do."

He nods, and after a few seconds of silence asks, "So you're pulling out?"

"We're pulling out—both Kenny and I."

"What's the plan?"

"In order to keep the speculation to a minimum, we're going to do an exclusive interview with Gospel Music Central together and make the announcement that the wedding is off," I say.

He scratches his head again. "Have you told the label?"

"They'll find out when the rest of the world does."

"But what about your recording deal? Aren't you worried that they'll find a reason to drop you?"

"Rick, my album is number one in Gospel music. They'd be crazy to drop me or Kenny. They'll get over it. They don't have a choice."

He lets out another sigh. I can tell that he respects my decision, but is having just as much of a hard time accepting it as I am myself. "All right. Is there anything that I can do to help?"

I grin. "Yes, there is. You can go down the street to the Chinese restaurant and replace that Teriyaki Chicken of mine that you just ate."

"Welcome back to Gospel Music Central. We're here today with Grammy award winning artists Davina Lacey and Kenny Kauffman. Before the break, we had the chance to talk to them about Davina's new album, *The Second Coming*, as well as Kenny's upcoming album that will be released later on this year. Of course, the real news that's on everyone's mind is your upcoming wedding. I've been told that you two have some important details about the wedding that you are exclusively sharing with us today. Am I right?"

Bright lights, a scenic backdrop, and several cameras fill the set of Gospel Music Central, a popular, inspirational music show. It is five days before the wedding, and time for Kenny and me to publically call it "splitsville." The show's host, Lauren Baker, has done a superb job of building our interview up to the big announcement. Kenny is sitting to my right and has been my rock throughout our time on set. My nerves are slowly getting the best of me, and I'm trying with all of my might not to have an emotional breakdown on screen. I have to get through this interview and say what I came here to say. I mentally pray for courage and offer the cameras the most sincere smile that I can muster up.

I take a deep breath. "Yes, Lauren. Kenny and I have come on the show to make an announcement about our wedding," I say, my heartbeat racing now that the moment is upon us. I look over at Kenny, hoping that he will take me out of my misery and make the announcement for me. To my relief, he smiles at me and speaks up.

"Lauren, we are grateful to all of our fans who have purchased our music and supported our relationship. It's been amazing to see how much people have rooted for us over the past two months since we announced our engagement. Unfortunately, I have a bit of bad news. Davina and I have decided not to get married this coming Saturday. The wedding has been cancelled."

She gasps. "Oh my! Okay, I wasn't expecting to hear that. Are you two breaking up?"

Feeling a bit more confident now that Kenny has "spilled the beans," I say, "Kenny and I care about each other very much and this decision has not been an easy one. But we feel that cancelling the wedding and taking a break as a couple is the best thing to do. We both want to focus on our separate ministries in music, and even more importantly, we both want to be sure of God's will in our lives as it relates to marriage."

"So you are breaking up?" Lauren asks again, looking for a confirmation.

Kenny grabs my hand, before nodding and saying, "We've decided to remain friends."

After the interview, Kenny and I walk out of the studio hand-in-hand to show our continued friendship and solidarity. I realize the people around us are watching us and even talking about us, but I've decided not to let it bother me anymore. I'm glad the lies are over and that I can have my life back. I know I need time to mend fences with God and get my spirit back in order.

"Thank you," I say to Kenny once we are out of the earshot of others. "I still don't understand why you've risked and sacrificed so much for me, but you're a great man and I will be praying for you."

He steps in front of me, preventing me from continuing to walk towards the parking lot. "I wasn't lying when I told Jill that I wanted to go out on a date with you. I got the chance to go out on many dates with you, so I think I've been paid in full for my sacrifice."

He's so kind. I know I'll miss him. "I don't want to say goodbye to you," I say.

"Then don't."

I shake my head. "I have to. If I don't my life will continue to be out-of-order. I just need time to get my head straight with God, you know?"

"I know."

We are having this awesome yet sorrowful moment when it's completely ruined by an annoying voice.

"I knew you two weren't going to make it. It's about time that you finally admitted it."

I turn my head to see Jill Sweet walking toward us with a silly grin on her face. I want to plead the blood of Jesus so bad over this devil, but I feel Kenny's hand squeezing mine, signaling me to remain cool.

Instead of replying to Jill, Kenny gently turns my head back to him with his other hand, looks into my eyes, and says, "All things are working together for our good."

He pulls me closer and plants the sweetest, most endearing kiss on my lips. I feel shiver run from my lips and down my spine. When he pulls away, I am speechless and weak in the knees. Thank God that Kenny is still holding on to me because it takes a few seconds for my legs to feel strong enough to walk on.

I realize that Jill is still standing there gawking at us. I take Kenny's lead and we walk past her as if she is a figment of our imaginations. As we move farther away from her, I hear her scream out Kenny's name, but he doesn't acknowledge her at all. Instead, like a gentleman, he walks me to my vehicle, opens and closes my car door, and makes certain I am safe, before letting me drive away.

Come Back to Me

Davina

I've been in a funk for months now, ever since the lie ended and reality resumed. I thought having a successful second album was what I wanted. I thought that my music ministry was everything I could ever hope for, but I was wrong—depressingly wrong. I didn't think someone I only knew for a matter of weeks could turn my life and heart upside down, but Kenny Kauffman is like a hurricane. He blew into my life, spun me around, and left me miles away from where I began. I feel like I don't know myself anymore because the thoughts that I'm having are nothing familiar to me. Love? Romance? Being focused on anything or anyone else other than my career? This has to be some cruel joke.

I find myself sitting in the dark, listening to old school love songs. Toni Braxton, Mariah Carey, SWV, Lisa Lisa and Cult Jam, and of course Janet Jackson. The ladies are all here, soothing my lonely heart with their vocal cords. Janet almost sends me over the edge with "Come Back to Me." How could a song written decades ago ring so true for me now?

I am about to replay Lisa Lisa's "All Cried Out," when Rick barges into my condo and turns off my stereo system.

"Hey!" I say to him, waving an ice cream covered spoon at him. I'm indulging in cherry vanilla and I don't appreciate his interference.

"So, you're really going to do this?" he asks me.

I greedily lick my spoon then plunge it deeply into the carton for another scoop. "Eat ice cream and listen to old CDs? You betcha."

"I'm talking about pining away over a guy you barely know," he says before coming over to me and snatching away the carton.

"Hey!" I say, holding on tightly to the spoon, which is all I have left now.

"I'm not going to let you fall apart like this."

I shrug my shoulders and insert the spoon into my mouth, savoring my final scoop of ice cream. What Rick doesn't know is that I have three more cartons in my fridge, and if he doesn't release the cherry vanilla soon, I'll just go and get the cartoon of butter pecan. "Give it back," I say with very little intimidation in my voice.

"No," he says while finding the lid and placing it on top of the carton. "Your trainer says that you've gained seven pounds and refuse to workout. You've got to snap out of this. We need to shoot a video for your new single this month, and if you don't shape up now, you're going to look sloppy."

"It's my body and seven pounds is not a big deal."

"Everything is a big deal in this industry," he says, sounding frustrated. He takes a seat on my plush wingback chair. "You said you wanted me to be both you manager and your cousin, so that's what I am doing. I'm trying to help you move forward in your career and to move past Kenny Kauffman. You said you didn't want to be with him, so why aren't you letting him go?"

I roll my eyes. "I didn't say that I didn't want to be with him. I said that we needed to go our separate ways."

"Isn't that the same thing?"

"No. I really care about Kenny, but the way we met, how we got engaged, all of it was so twisted. How could God bless a relationship that was so screwed up? As much as it's difficult to do, sometimes we have to step back from our mistakes if we really hope to make things right."

Rick shakes his head as if he disagrees. "God can bless whatever He chooses."

"That's true," I say, "but He is also calling us to a higher standard. We have to be examples to the world. If Kenny and I just got together in the midst of all of that scandal, our love story and ultimately testimony would have been built on the foundation of sin. Rehashing our true story would have caused us to either have to lie to make our relationship seem perfect, or admit that instead of repenting, we just dismissed our shortcomings and did whatever we wanted to do. That's how the world lives their lives, but believers must follow a different path."

"A path of self-denial?"

"No, Rick. A path of submission. I have submitted to God my feelings and desires about Kenny. As much as I want to force a relationship with him, I have to have faith that if being with Kenny is a part of God's will for my life, at some point in the future, He will bring us back together. And in the meantime, I can and will indulge in ice cream and sad love songs."

Rick puts the half eaten carton of ice cream on the coffee table in front of him. "You have a point—about the God stuff, not the ice cream. Most people I know wouldn't care. They would see it as divine intervention that you two met in the first place."

I eye the ice cream, wondering if I make a leap for it, will he snatch it away before I can get to it. I don't think I'm faster than him, so I reject the idea. "Nope, that was label intervention. The divine part was that God allowed it. Just because He allowed it doesn't mean we still aren't accountable for our actions."

"Davina, you're pretty wise. You should put all of that in a song."

"Trust me, I'm working on it. I won't let anything I've been through be wasted."

"Good. Oh, I meant to tell you. Nora has scheduled you for another interview on the Mitch Davis Morning Show. It's next Thursday at eight. At least that's one good thing that came out of this whole ordeal. Hiring Nora as your new publicist was extremely smart."

I nod. "I should have had my own publicist from the start instead of trusting my image in the hands of the label. Nora's a good woman and she'll do right by me."

"Is she still working with Kenny too?"

"I think so, but I try not to discuss Kenny with her. If he's her client, I don't want to make her feel awkward or caught in the middle between the two of us."

"I understand," he says then stands. He picks up the container. "I need to get going, but I'm confiscating your ice cream, and I want to see you with your trainer, bright and early tomorrow morning. Do you hear me?"

"Loud and clear," I say, and salute him as if he's in the military. Nonetheless, the minute he shuts my front door, I race into the kitchen and pull the butter pecan ice cream out of the freezer. Patience is a virtue.

"Welcome back to the Mitch Davis Morning Show. We are here in the studio again with the lovely Davina Lacey—songwriter, singer, rapper, Grammy-awarding winning artist, Billboard topping singer, multi-platinum recording artist, and the list of accolades goes on and on."

I smile and say, "Thanks, Mitch. All glory goes to God." It feels good to be back on radio, promoting my music. I haven't eaten ice cream in three days so my mood is certainly improving.

"And I guess I left out humble. So, how have you been, Davina? You know, the last time we had you on here, you and Kenny Kauffman were supposed to be getting married. Unfortunately, that didn't happen, and we're sure that was a hard decision for you. How have you been since then?"

I prepared myself in advance for questions about Kenny, so I am unfazed by Mitch bringing him up. "It was a difficult decision and Kenny's a great guy, which made it even harder to do. But it was the right thing to do, and both Kenny and I made the choice together. So although it hasn't been easy, I've been moving forward thanks to the grace of God."

"Well, we're glad that you have good things to say about Kenny because we have a little surprise for you. Kenny Kauffman is here in the studio. Let's bring him in and reunite these two right here on the Mitch Davis Morning Show."

I turn in my chair and see Kenny being led into the room. I quickly glance over to the hallway's window where I'd left Rick and see that Nora is now standing there with him. They both offer me bright, meddlesome smiles and wave at me innocently. I glare at them, but they seem unconcerned by my visual threat because they continue to smile back at me. Kenny takes the seat next to me and I instantly feel an unexplainable heat fill the space between us. I slowly move my eyes upward to make contact with his, and the moment they do, my breath escapes me.

"Kenny, man, it's good to see you. How are you?" Mitch says into his microphone. I'm pulled back into the moment, realizing that we're still on live radio.

"I'm good, Mitch. Blessed. Thanks for having me on the show today."

"It's my pleasure. So, from what I've heard, this is the first time that you two have seen each other in four months. Is this true?"

"Yeah, it's been about that long," Kenny answers.

"How does it feel to see her again?"

Kenny gazes at me. "It feels good. She looks gorgeous, but she always does."

I blush at the compliment and look away.

"Sounds like you've really missed her," Mitch says.

"I have, Mitch. I've missed her like crazy."

"What about you, Davina? Have you missed Kenny?"

I glance back at Kenny and see nothing but sincerity in his eyes. In the past, I would have denied my feelings, especially knowing that millions of listeners are tuned into this very private moment, but I can no long hide the desire of my heart. "Ridiculously," I say.

"If you all have never witnessed love, you're going to witness it here this morning on the Mitch Davis Morning Show. Kenny, my man, do your thing."

Kenny scoots off his chair and kneels down on the floor. A gasp escapes my mouth because it appears as if he's about to propose. My eyes quickly dart back to the window where Rick and Nora are looking all tearful and sappy.

I turn my attention back to Kenny who says, "Davina, I know that we agreed to go our separate ways so that we could know God's will. Over the past months, I've prayed constantly for God to reveal His will to me, and the answer is always the same—you. Maybe our relationship didn't begin the right way, but that doesn't mean that God can't turn what was meant for bad into something good, something beautiful."

He pulls a platinum band from his pocket that looks more like a wedding ring than an engagement ring. "Davina Lacey, I am on bended knee, offering you not an engagement ring, but a promise ring. I promise to get to know everything I can about you, and to allow myself to fall head-over-heels in love with you. And I promise to make you my wife when you're ready to take that step with me. I promise to protect you and to cover you spiritually, mentally, and physically. Will you accept my promise?"

I am choked up, but I manage to croak out, "Yes." He places the band on my ring finger, stands up, and pulls me up with him. Gently, he lift my chin with his index finger and kisses me like a man who knows exactly who he loves. He loves me, and even better, I love him, too.

"And there you have it, folks. Kevina is back, y'all!" Mitch says with enthusiasm, causing Kenny and me to burst into laughter. "From the looks of these two, I estimate the wedding will be back on very, *very* soon. We have to go to break and pay some bills, but when we come back, we'll have another inspirational minute from Dr. Yolanda Morrow."

THE WIFE-TO-BE SERIES
NOVELLA #1

Wife without a Ring

Shawna Claxton couldn't care less about capturing the coveted promotion at her job or having a fulfilling career. There is only one position she wants and has waited her entire life to get—to be a housewife. Though her friends think she is old fashioned, her current beau, NFL kicker Andy Tate, loves the idea. But when Andy finally proposes—in an unromantic way and without a ring—Shawna finds herself engaged in a very public battle between getting the man and getting the bling.

Wife Insurance

Wealthy resort owner, Cole Haven, is supposed to get married on Christmas to Violet, the woman he's been engaged to for the past five years. Yet, the same problem that has kept him from committing to the ceremony once again gives him an impossible case of cold feet—his distrust for women due to the actions of his ex-wife, Sophia. When Sophia hits him with an unreasonable ultimatum a month before his holiday wedding, and Violet is unwilling to compromise this Christmas, Cole will have to choose between taking a leap of faith or using the past as an indicator for what the future holds. If only he had a bit of wife insurance to guarantee him that marriage to Violet won't be the second biggest mistake of his life...

Wife Next Door

Felicia Jefferson and Morris Bryson have been best friends since childhood. Morris has always appreciated Felicia for standing by his side through his bouts with a lifelong disease. At age 16, they made a pact that if neither of them were married by the time she turned 35, they would marry one another. As fate would have it, at 36, his chronic illness worsens and he attempts to cash-in on his agreement with Felicia, wanting to experience marriage before he dies. As much as Felicia desires to grant her sick friend's request, marrying Morris means breaking up with her boyfriend of two years and sacrificing her plans to marry for love. Is a lifetime of friendship strong enough to survive an unexpected proposal, sympathy marriage, and a life-threatening disease?

About the Author

A'ndrea J. Wilson is the author of over twenty books, including the award-winning Wife 101 series. A'ndrea dates her writing career back to high school where she majored in creative writing at Rochester, New York's School of the Arts. After graduation, she pursued careers in psychology and education, earning a Master's degree in Marriage and Family Counseling and a Ph.D. in Educational Leadership. An avid reader, she could never shake her passion for books, which eventually led to her penning her first manuscript. Her continuously growing body of faith-based work primarily focuses on integrating her clinical background and interest in relationship development with fiction; however, she also writes supernatural thrillers under the pseudonym Janell. In addition to writing, A'ndrea is a college professor and the president of Divine Garden Press, an independent publishing company based in Georgia. For more information, please visit her at www.andreawilsononline.com or www.wife101.com

www.ingramcontent.com/pod-product-compliance
Lightning Source LLC
Chambersburg PA
CBHW020627130626
46552CB00003B/1115